Congratulations on your new
lion! We know you ordered a
kitten, but we ran out of those.

Luckily, a lion is practically
the same thing!

Caring for your lion is easy.
Just follow this handy guide.

# Caring for
# Your Lion

·······································

by Tammi Sauer
illustrated by Troy Cummings

STERLING CHILDREN'S BOOKS
New York

**Pop!**

**STEP 2**

Locate the enclosed feather. Keep it handy in case of an emergency.

Try very hard NOT to look like a zebra.
Or a gazelle. Or a bunny.

(See Diagram A.)

A.

If you ignored STEP 3, you are probably sitting inside a lion right now. No problem! Simply use your feather.

(See Diagrams B, C, D, and E.)

**B.**

**C.**

**D.**

**E.**

**STEP 5**

Order ten large pizzas and promptly feed your lion.

When your lion accidentally swallows the pizza delivery guy, you know what to do!

Potty train your lion.
It's a cinch with the
Deluxe Lion Potty Pack.

(Some assembly required. See Diagram F.)

F.

5W

300 lbs.

TOOLS
NEEDED:

LITTER ×50

SCOOP-DE-DOO
CAT
LITTER
100 lbs.

## STEP 7

Provide your lion with space to play.

Your lion loves to nap. Be ready for him to doze off just about anywhere.

ROOOOO

**STEP 9** Give your lion an occasional treat—especially when he does something good.

At bath time, fill the tub with equal parts water and lion. Then add a smidge of bubble bath. Be sure to have your camera ready for some adorable photos!

# STEP 11

Post-bath, your lion is half his normal size.
Do. Not. Panic.
Simply grab a blow dryer and get busy.
(Expect a teensy bit of shedding.)

**STEP 12**

At the end of a full day,
your lion is sleepy.
Prepare a cozy bed for him.

Realize your lion is the purrrrr-fect pet for you.

**For Mason. —T. S.**

**For Edie: the fiercest, furriest, fang-iest member of the family. —T. C.**

**STERLING CHILDREN'S BOOKS**
New York

An Imprint of Sterling Publishing Co., Inc.
1166 Avenue of the Americas
New York, NY 10036

ISBN 978-1-4549-1609-3

Distributed in Canada by Sterling Publishing Co., Inc.
c/o Canadian Manda Group, 664 Annette Street
Toronto, Ontario, Canada M6S 2C8
Distributed in the United Kingdom by GMC Distribution Services
Castle Place, 166 High Street, Lewes, East Sussex, England BN7 1XU
Distributed in Australia by NewSouth Books
45 Beach Street, Coogee, NSW 2034, Australia

For information about custom editions, special sales, and premium and corporate purchases,
please contact Sterling Special Sales at 800-805-5489 or specialsales@sterlingpublishing.com.

Manufactured in China.

Lot #:
2  4  6  8  10  9  7  5  3  1
02/17

www.sterlingpublishing.com

The artwork for this book was created digitally.
Art direction and design by Jo Obarowski.